A CASE IN ANY CASE

DETECTIVE · GORDON

A CASE IN ANY CASE

ULF NILSSON
ILLUSTRATED BY GITTE SPEE

GECKO PRESS

A mysterious scrabbler

It was a dark autumn night in the forest.
An eerie wind howled through the trees.
An owl hooted in reply.

   At the edge of the woods was a small police
station where the lights were always on.
A small haven of light in the darkness, a place
where you could ask for help at any time.

If you went inside—the door was always unlocked—
you found yourself at once in the large police room.

On the left was a hat stand with two stylish police
hats. To the right was a glass cupboard with a black
pistol inside it and a terrifying baton. The cupboard
was always locked. In front of it was a great big desk
with an old-fashioned stamp on it.

A little further in was the old prison, still with its
barred door. But for now this was where the police
chief slept.

If you crept in there you'd see the chief still snuggled
up in bed. Mouth open, snoring lightly with soft little
sighs. The bed was large and Police Chief Buffy was
small, like a cinnamon bun beneath the cover.

Buffy was a mouse, zero years old. She was the one looking after the police station while old Police Chief Gordon was away. Taking a break—a very long break actually…

Suddenly the stillness of the night was broken. Someone was scrabbling at the windowpane. Scrabble, scrabble. As if a hungry animal were trying to get inside.

Buffy woke at once and sat up in bed.

Outside the window, a large shapeless thing was scrambling around in the garden. Grunts and sighs could be heard. Still in her pink nightdress, Buffy ran on tiptoe to the door.

Now, through the other window, she glimpsed the large dark head of the terrible thing. Or was it two things?

She gathered her courage, opened the door, and asked into the night:

"What have we here then?"

No one answered. It was quiet. Far away, the owl hooted.

"In the name of the law!" said Buffy.

Complete silence. She sniffed to catch a scent, a clue.

Nothing—although she could detect a hint of her old friend Gordon. All his old things still smelled of him,

of course. Or she might have been imagining it.
Because at that moment Buffy was missing Gordon.

She was suddenly frightened. A small mouse alone
in the big forest. The wind howled and her tail was
ice-cold. Her whiskers trembled. Maybe she should call
the police. Then she remembered: she *was* the police.

Buffy stared out into the darkness. She was afraid.
But she was a police officer who always did what she
had to do. In that regard she was very brave.

She called out: "Welcome to the police station.
We're here to help you..."

Her voice was a little shaky.

Then she went back inside. She put on her fine
police hat and sat down at the large desk. A little
mouse in a pink nightie. A big hat with a gold badge.
A big stamp in her hand.

She bravely hummed a song she was meaning to write. A marching song for police on parade.

She wrote a note about what had happened:

A mysterious scrabbler scrabbling.
Gordon must be called in.

Buffy had been working on her writing all summer. She could do it very well now. But "scrabbler" was a word she'd never written before.

She took out the stamp. Placed it on the paper. Moved it a little to the right. Moved it a little to the left. Pushed it with all her might. Kla-dunk.

When morning came and the sun shone in through the window, she was still sitting at the desk. She hadn't had much sleep that night!

Buffy made a cup of tea and ate her morning cake, a walnut ball, which tasted wonderful. She took an extra walnut too. Eating nuts made her full of energy.

Then she washed her face, dipping the tips of her fingers in a little water and polishing her nose. She took off her nightie and put on her everyday clothes. She put the police hat back on the hat stand. Then she set off walking briskly through the forest.

These days, Gordon was living in a little house by the lake. A wisp of smoke curled from the chimney. It looked very peaceful. On the veranda was a stripy deck chair. Gordon's black raincoat was hanging from a hook. Buffy knocked on the door and opened it.

Gordon wasn't home. The gigantic bed took up most of the room. It was nicely made. The woodstove glowed with the remains of a fire. A teapot, a cup, and a book lay open on the bedside table. There were a lot of cake crumbs. Buffy sniffed them. Hmm, Gordon had also eaten walnut balls for breakfast. The cup was empty. The teapot was a little warm. He'd eaten breakfast a short while ago then gone out on an errand.

I'll wait for him, Buffy decided.

She looked at the book: *Funny Stories about Mice and Toads*. Gordon had just finished a story that went like this:

There was a baby mouse who caught sight of a bat.
"Look, Mother, an angel!"

She giggled. A bat is a mouse with wings that can fly. A flying mouse! She could picture Gordon roaring with laughter, making his big belly wobble as he lay there reading and eating walnut balls.

She missed him. It's not good for police to be alone, she thought gloomily. Two police think twice as well as one. Two police are twice as brave.

Then she sat down in the deck chair on the veranda. She heard a cheerful song.

Bomba bomba, on a walk
In kindergarten we sing and talk.
Bomba bomba BOMBA!

It was all the forest children from the kindergarten on an expedition. Buffy saluted the teacher mouse at the front of the line. The children all wore flowery tops and backpacks. They walked in a long line and jabbered. She couldn't help hearing what they said:

A baby toad: I'm going to slide in the mud, I'm going to…

A baby mole: Teacher, I've lost my backpack.

Teacher: I've got it!

A baby rabbit: Then we can build a house to live in.

A baby squirrel: We can be farmers and grow nuts…

Baby rabbit: Nuts, yuck. Carrots are better.
And we should plant cakes!

How they chattered! Buffy leaned back and waited.
And waited. Eventually she had to go back to work
at the police station.

She thought: Why would anyone scrabble at the police
station windows late at night? And then just disappear?

And where was Gordon?

A wise police officer

Gordon sat fishing beside the stream. His float bounced on the water. Under the surface he could see small fish nibbling at the piece of bread.

"Hi, little fishes," said Gordon.

Gordon was taking a break. A long break. Hmm, he was maybe even retired. He had been a police chief all his life. Towards the end he had been feeling very tired and worn out. All he'd wanted to do was to eat cakes and sleep. But now he was starting to feel brighter.

In recent weeks he had thought a lot about his life. A life of constant police service, with a beautiful police hat and magnificent stamp to kla-dunk when he made important decisions.

He hadn't had time for anything else.

Now he was sitting here with his fishing rod working out what to do.

The sun began to set. He pulled up the bait. With no fish, of course.

"Hey there, small fishes," he said. "Might see you in the morning."

He went home humming a small song.

Two young mice came towards him on the track. They said hello politely, and he saluted out of habit. No, he mustn't, he wasn't a police officer now!

Police Chief Gordon was no longer chief. He was simply Gordon.

He could hear the mice talking.

"That new police officer is very smart and brave," said one. "Best in the world!"

"Very stylish in her hat," said the other.

Gordon went into his house. He ate four cakes, but they didn't taste as good as usual. He leafed through his book of jokes. No, they weren't funny. He felt dejected.

"I've been a police officer my whole life," he said to himself. "I know all there is to know about police work in forests and fields."

He felt a little brighter and ate two more cakes. There, they tasted better now!

"It's hard to be in the police, because a police officer mustn't think of himself," he said. "He must think mostly about the other animals in his district. A police officer never gets angry, but is always understanding. The most important thing is that all the forest animals are happy and safe."

And he ate a few more delicious cakes.

But now he felt irritated by the two young mice.

"Best in the world!" "Stylish!" Hmph!

There's so much to being a police officer, he thought. You have to be there at the little police station. Ready to receive anyone who's unhappy.

Maybe a squirrel who's had his nuts stolen. Always sympathizing and offering a cup of tea! Listening and trying to understand the squirrel's convoluted story. Always bearing in mind the missing nuts.

Then investigating and looking for tracks. Phew! Stalking magpies and spying on ferrets.

Lying in bed and thinking. Pondering all the suspects and figuring out who is the culprit.

And last of all, cracking down on those who behave badly.

Thinking up some modest but effective punishment. Suitable: small but persuasive!

It wasn't enough to go around looking stylish in your hat! Ha!

He rummaged for a piece of paper and began to write.

A wise police officer is never angry and always thinks of others first.

Now all he had to do was to stamp the paper and put it in the drawer for important notes.

But he didn't have a stamp. Or a drawer. Things couldn't go on like this. It wasn't possible that he'd solved his last case.

"I want to be Chief Detective again!" he wailed. "I want to work on a case."

I'll have to go over and spy again tonight, he thought.

It was raining, so, as he'd done the night before, he put on his black raincoat and rain hat, and his rubber boots...

Big, strong police

And so night came again to the police station. Buffy felt anxious, in case the scrabbler turned up again.

I should be as brave and wise as Gordon, she thought. Except that I actually am brave and wise!

Buffy pulled out the drawer where important notes were kept. *No crime, no punishment* was written on a piece of paper, carefully stamped. *Everyone should always be allowed to play with everybody* said another. *It is permitted to be both nice and un-nice—as long as it is un-nasty.*

Typical Gordon to be simple in a complicated way.

"But I can write things like that too!"

Buffy tried to imagine she was Gordon. She puffed up her cheeks to make herself rounder. She pulled down the corners of her mouth and stared hard to make her eyes bigger. She checked in the mirror. Ha, she looked like Gordon now—but a thin Gordon.

She put on a nightie and stuffed a pillow inside.
Ah, that was it.

She gobbled some cakes and stood in front of the
mirror. She imitated Gordon's voice.

"Gruff, gruff. Nothing harmful shall happen in our
police district, gruff. The most important thing for
police is that everyone is safe! Everyone should be
happy in the forest, come safely home at the end of
the day and enjoy a sound sleep. Not until all are asleep
in their beds at night can the police be satisfied. Gruff.
This is the most important goal of the police!"

Buffy began thinking about owls and bats.

"Some animals are up in the night and don't go
to sleep until morning. Hmm."

Buffy wrote:

Everyone should sleep happy.
Good night! Good morning!

She put her stamp on the paper.

Moved it a little to the right, a little to the left and
a little to the right again. Kla-dunk. She had stamped
a new piece of wisdom! Likely to be true, even if it

sounded a little perplexing and thin compared to others in the drawer.

Oh, how she missed Gordon! Everything was much more fun when there were two police friends.

Gruff-gruff was the sound she made nibbling the last two pieces of cake. A little tear of longing rolled onto the paper.

Then she went to bed.

Maybe I can find Gordon in the morning, she thought. I just hope nothing happens in the night...

An even darker and more daunting autumn night fell in the woods. The wind howled horribly. And when the owl hooted—*whoo!*—how eerie it was.

Buffy lay with her eyes wide open, peering all around. She hated these terrible autumn nights when the wind blustered about, making the whole police station creak. But at last she slept. Snore, sigh.

In the middle of the night she woke to a sound and sat straight up in bed.

Something was walking around the police station. There were squelching steps. The black shadow of a formless thing. More squelching. And then scrabbling at the window.

The terrible scrabbler was back! Or two of them!

Buffy shot under the bed, pulled the pillow after her and hid behind it.

But then she remembered that she was the police and must behave *accordingly*. She crept out again and went bravely to the door.

"Who's scrabbling at my window?" she asked. Alas, her voice was a little squeaky.

She heard footsteps outside, squelching away. So she opened the door. No one there! Only darkness and rain and the howling wind. Her tail stuck out like an arrow in fear and her bottom lip began to quiver. Was that a faint whiff of toad, or was she imagining it again?

Buffy closed the door quickly and sat down at the writing desk. She drummed her fingers nervously on the desk.

To give herself courage, she began to hum the police parade march as she wrote it:

Here come the forest police, ha ha.
The biggest, strongest police! Tra-la-la.

But she didn't feel any calmer. She *had to* get help.

"I'm going to Gordon's now!" she said out loud.

She dressed warmly and hunted for the lantern. At the door she stopped and looked at the pistol. Should she take it with her? No, they must never take the pistol,

never never. She had promised Gordon. But she took Gordon's police hat.

Then she set off into the darkness with her scarf tucked up around her nose.

At Gordon's small house the window was dark. She stepped onto the veranda.

The wind seized the deck chair and made it flap like a striped ghost. She didn't notice the wet boots and raincoat hanging on the hook.

She opened the door.

It was so still and calm inside. Warm and safe. Gordon lay in the big bed. Was he asleep? His round head stuck out from the cover. His big mouth was open.

She stood listening to him. He snored in a friendly, rumbling sort of way. Buffy felt both happy and a little moved.

Gordon suddenly opened his eyes.

"What? Buffy!" he said. "My dear Police Chief Buffy!"

"Chief Detective Gordon," she said. "I have a troublesome case under way and I need your help.

You said I only had to whistle, *hwee hwee hwee*, and
you'd be there…"

"Oh, I'm so glad you've come. Is it very urgent?
Or do we have time for cakes?"

Gordon stepped out of bed, made the tea, and set
out seven small pear cakes. The house wasn't large.
The bed didn't leave much room for other furniture,
so they sat on the edge of the bed and drank tea.

Buffy outlined the frightening and mysterious goings-on.

Gordon blushed a little; there were things he needed to tell Buffy. He hummed. But oh dear, it was a bit embarrassing...

"Why don't you stay here tonight," said Gordon. "You can lie at the bottom of the bed. In the morning we'll sort it all out."

"Thank you!" said Buffy. "But what have you been doing all summer? What were you doing yesterday?"

"Fishing," said Gordon. "I've been fishing every day and thinking about life. Well, I don't use a hook of course. I just feed the small friendly fishes in the stream. But being retired is actually quite boring..."

It had always sounded good in theory, but really it was boring, boring, he thought.

"I'm so glad you've come, Buffy! I can read you some funny mouse stories before we sleep," Gordon continued. "And tomorrow we'll go to the police station. I'll be interested to see what it looks like these days. Hmm, yes."

So Buffy crept down into a corner of the bed. Gordon read a funny story. It was a little hard to hear what he was saying because he kept laughing to himself. His belly bounced and the bed shook.

There were some mice being chased by a cat. But one of them called out, Woof woof woof. And the cat got—HE HE HEE—really scared and ran away. Then the mouse said: "It's so good to be able to speak—HA HA HAA—other languages."

"It was dog language, you see," Gordon chuckled.

"I get it," said Buffy.

"And have you heard this one? *How does a toad eat a fox?*"

But Buffy had fallen asleep. Gordon turned out the light.

"Goodnight, goodnight, my best friend," he said.

Two children go missing!

In the morning the sun was shining again and the air was still. It was a wonderful day for two police friends to wander through the forest. Both were wearing their fine gold police hats. They were going to the police station for breakfast.

On the way, Buffy couldn't help thinking about the mysterious scrabbler. Or scrabblers, because there could be more than one.

"He, she, or they are very flabby and squelchy," she said.

"Ah!" exclaimed Gordon.

"They looked really horrible," said Buffy.

"Ah-ha," Gordon murmured.

"I wonder if he, she, or they wanted to say something," said Buffy.

"Call it the ghost," suggested Gordon. "It's too awkward saying *he, she, or they*...the ghost!"

"Gosh," said Buffy, who didn't like the ghost one little bit. "But if the ghost wanted to frighten someone, he, she, or they shouldn't just disappear..."

Gordon looked at her.

"A ghost ought to carry on and say *boo! hoo!* or flap its sheet..."

"Is that right?" said Gordon, who would have preferred to talk about the breakfast ahead of them.

"The ghost didn't *want* to frighten anyone," continued Buffy. "It wanted to spy!"

They both had a think. Gordon thought about how he needed to put a stop to this talk. He thought so hard that he had to sit down and rest by a tree. Then he stretched out. He thought best when he was lying down. But it didn't seem to help.

"Maybe the ghost wanted to spy on *you*," said Buffy. "Maybe it was an old enemy who wanted to tell you off because you caught him. Maybe it was the old fox who was angry because you kicked him out of the forest that time."

Gordon looked doubtful and shook his head.

"What if the fox is back? Actually the old crow reckoned the fox might come back," said Buffy. "But... it didn't smell of fox. It smelled just a little like you."

Gordon sat up.

"Do I have a smell?"

Buffy reminded him that she was a master of scents. Gordon smelled of freshly made bed, cakes, and a funny book. It was probably an old Gordon smell that had lingered...

As they sat, things were going on in the field. A little way away the kindergarten children were setting out. First the teacher, then the little ones scattering out behind her. Strangely enough, there was no cheerful song. Had something happened?

"Do you know how happy I am?" said Gordon.

The kindergarten children were looking among the bushes and grass. The teacher was running back and forth, hither and thither.

"I was so glad when you came and woke me," he continued.

"You were glad to be woken up?"

The teacher waved her arms. Some of the children
began to cry. She called something, but Gordon and
Buffy couldn't hear what.

Gordon thought he was a police officer again.
He patted his police hat.

Buffy was also thinking—about the fox. She was
worried that he had come back and wanted to eat
Gordon up. How could she protect her police friend?
She thought and thought. And then she had it.

A flour bomb! All she had to do
was make an ordinary flour bomb
before night. Simple!

The kindergarten teacher began to hop up and down. All the little ones were wailing. And the teacher shouted at the top of her voice:

"Police! Police! Help! Two children have gone missing!"

The two police leaped to their feet and ran towards her.

This was the worst thing that could happen. The most horrible. Anything else was trifling by comparison.

Because so what if nuts were stolen? It was only a matter of putting them back.

And what if someone was being teased? They only needed an apology.

What did it matter if someone was scrabbling around mysteriously? They could simply ask the ghost to go back to bed.

But two children missing! That was so terrible it made most people cry.

And Chief Detective Gordon had tears in his eyes. But he quickly took out a large handkerchief, blew his nose with a snort and wiped it. Now he must be professional, a real police officer working on a new case.

Chief Detective Buffy's heart began to beat wildly. She thought of the two little babies crying. She thought

about the fox licking his lips… No, away with such
thoughts! First everything must be thoroughly
investigated.

The teacher wept and all the little ones whimpered.

Chief Detective Buffy realized that they must stay
calm and think carefully. Wails and whimpers, sobs and
sighs, noisy nose-blowing and pounding hearts were of
no help. First they all needed to calm down.

Buffy sat on a stone and began to sing her new song
in a clear voice. The words came all by themselves.

Look, the forest police are here!
The brave police are always near.
Forest animals everywhere,
Put yourselves into their care.
They keep the forest free of harm,
So you can sleep in peace and calm.
Call on them and never fear:
The forest police will soon appear.

Oh, it was good! And all the young ones gathered around her and stopped sniffling. Gordon put his handkerchief away in his pocket. The teacher cleared her throat.

"Tell us calmly and clearly what has happened," Buffy said to the teacher.

"I will take notes," said Gordon.

And the mouse teacher explained that she had gone out with the entire kindergarten in the morning. There were twelve little ones. Baby toads, baby crows, magpie babies, squirrel babies, little rabbits, and moles…

They had planned to go to the big field across the big stream. But the grass was so wet they had turned back.

When they returned to the little field there were only ten children. Everyone had looked and called and howled.

Two youngsters missing, Gordon wrote in his notebook.

"Which ones have you lost?" asked Buffy.

"A squirrel called Evert," said the teacher. "A little philosopher who goes about in a dream. And a young rabbit called Karen. Quite a rascal."

"Hmm," said Gordon, thinking how easily a small dreamer can go astray.

"Hmm," said Buffy, thinking how easily a young rascal can be caught up in an adventure.

The young ones were wearing flowery tops and backpacks and each had a walking stick.

"Have they left anything behind?" asked Buffy.

"No, everything's gone! Tops, backpacks, and sticks."

That's a shame, thought Buffy. Otherwise I could have tracked them by smell…

"Is there any item that smells of Evert or Karen?" asked Gordon.

No answer.

"Does anyone have anything that belonged to Evert or Karen?" Gordon clarified. "Because Buffy is very good at following the scents of missing…"

A small toad came forward and opened his hand. There was a piece of white cloth taped around a cone. A wide mouth was painted on the cloth.

"What is this?" asked Gordon.

"An old man," said the little toad. "A happy man. Evert made it and gave it to me."

A scent to follow! Buffy pressed forward and looked at the wrinkled cone man in the small sweaty hand.

She sniffed. Many smells were mingled in the cloth. Spilled juice, crayons, glue, nuts, a book, dust, an old stick, and cake crumbs—the little man smelled a little too much of everything. Buffy tried to track the scent, but in the wet grass all the smells ran together. She had to give up.

After that they all went around calling *Evert!* and *Karen!*

They looked one last time through bushes and up into trees, under tussocks and down holes.

The police chiefs wanted to go straight back to the kindergarten classroom to make further enquiries.

The matter was urgent. Two children really were missing!

Aatan ap?

Two big rabbits, who happened to be passing, stopped in the field to watch them all hurrying back to the kindergarten.

"Now the police are taking care of everything," the teacher told the little ones, "so we have nothing to worry about."

Look, the forest police are here! the children sang happily. *The brave police are always near.*

It was time for fruit at the big table. All the children shared a banana—except for the baby mole, who was given a dry beetle.

Two chairs were empty.

Gordon and Buffy went quietly around and investigated, on the hunt for clues.

They found Evert's and Karen's photos above the hooks where they hung their coats.

Evert was looking up at clouds in his picture. On his shelf was a pile of clean underpants. Yes, sometimes he had an accident.

The photo of Karen was of a blurred rabbit; she couldn't keep still while the photo was taken. Her shelf had a pile of extra socks. Yes, sometimes she forgot that you get wet going straight through puddles.

Buffy sniffed, but the clothes smelled only of soap. Gordon peeled the photos from the wall. They might be needed.

In the playroom each young one had their own box. Evert's box was filled to the brim with cone people. Sad cones, angry cones, happy cones with hats made from cardboard, and a cross cone who'd lost a hat. In Karen's box were lots of crinkled drawings. The problem was that you couldn't tell what they were of.

"Orange stripes and sausages?" suggested Buffy. "And different kinds of dots?"

They had to find clues! They had to understand how the children usually played. Then maybe they could figure out where they'd gone.

"If not…" said Buffy.

All the little ones had finished eating and poured into the playroom.

The teacher had a headache from all the excitement and went to lie down for a moment.

"Where's the farmer book?" the children asked.

Gordon shook his head. The farmer book? He hadn't seen such a thing.

"Farmer book!" the children ran around calling, as if the book could hear them. "Farmer boo-ook!"

"I hope nothing terrible has happened," Buffy said.

"Shh!" said Gordon.

The police friends decided to speak their secret language so they wouldn't frighten the young ones unnecessarily. The secret language of police was the A language. "Tha sacrat languaga af palaca was tha a-languaga."

A little awkward but it worked pretty well.

"A hapa thay havant baan aatan ap," said Buffy.

"Aatan ap?" Gordon was puzzled.

"Eaten up," whispered Buffy. "Atan ap by tha fax!"

They fell silent. An icy feeling shivered through them. Maybe there was something in what the crow had said, Gordon thought. What if the fox was back and hungry and…

"Na, A cannat avan thank that. Harrabla!"

"What?"

"I can't even think that," whispered Buffy.

All the little ones had stopped calling for the book. They stared in surprise at the two police who spoke so strangely.

"Halla, chaldran!" Buffy said and waved to them. "I mean, hello, children!"

Gordon thought carefully. Could the fox have eaten them?

"Na," he said. "Taps, backpacks, and stacks ara alsa gana!"

Now Buffy hardly understood a word. But yes! Tops, backpacks, and sticks were also gone. If the fox had eaten the children, he would have spat out the backpacks or at least the walking sticks. He couldn't be so hungry as to eat everything.

"Bat parhaps ha has haddan tha backpacks!" said Gordon.

"Haddan?" said Buffy.

"Hidden…in a bush," whispered Gordon.

"Than wa mast laak vara carafalla. Look!"

"First I need to ask the children some questions," Gordon said in normal language.

Hmm, he thought. I don't actually know how to interrogate small animals. It's so long since I was small myself…

Gordon went and sat on the reading sofa. He coughed and straightened his gold police hat.

"Listen up, you youngsters!" he said, using his police voice. "Come here immediately and sit down so I can interrogate you!"

The little ones looked terrified and ran instead to the opposite corner of the room. They looked shyly at the floor.

"Does any one know where the missing children might have gone?"

All the young ones tried to hide behind each other. The little mole Elliot happened to end up in front. He blushed and shook his head timidly. Buffy couldn't understand why Gordon sounded so stern.

"Did either of the youngsters talk about running away?" asked Gordon in a powerful voice.

The baby mole crept between the legs of the others. The cluster of little ones trembled and a baby hedgehog ended up at the front. He stuck out all his prickles, so they could scarcely hear his tiny *no* from inside.

"Can you tell me any more about the missing youngsters?"

A little shriek of fear went through the mob of children and they all ran to hide under the dining table.

"They're certainly rather shy," said Gordon.

Hmm, he thought. That was a complete failure. I don't know how to deal with these little ones.

Buffy didn't know what to say.

"Na wa mast saarch!" she said instead. "Search!"

They went out of the kindergarten and away to the little field.

"At was daffacalt ta spaak ta tham. A dadn't andastand axactla what A saad masalf…"

Gordon looked at Buffy sadly.

"We can stop speaking the secret language now we're alone," he said. "We must organize our search."

49

New ~~interrogation~~ game

The chiefs summoned all the animals in the forest.

First came Evert's father and mother, two nervous squirrels who stood clutching hands and sniffling anxiously. And Karen's mother with fourteen unruly babies. She was quite used to one of them disappearing now and then. They always came back in the end, she said.

Buffy ran after moles digging deep tunnels in the earth. She rushed after mice collecting nuts in the hazel bushes. Gordon shouted so all the rabbits and hares came out of the thickets. Buffy whistled so that birds came flying—though there were not so many birds. It was autumn and some had already flown south while others were packing and didn't have time.

But there were one hundred and eighty animals to help search. In the air. In the trees. On the ground. And under the ground.

"We must search every corner for the children," said Gordon. "And see if we can find any trace of them."

He showed the photos of Evert and Karen.

The animals took each other's hands and went off two by two. Such a long, meandering chain couldn't overlook a little squirrel who sat pondering. Or a blurry rabbit.

"This is what we call a search party line," said Gordon.

A couple of animals had no place in the line. One rabbit started to gather blankets, which could be useful when they found the missing children. A mouse went and fetched hot chocolate.

A squirrel hunted out funny
books to cheer up Karen
and Evert.

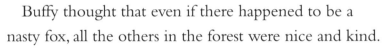

Everybody helped.
One hundred and eighty
friendly forest animals wanted
to do all they could to help.

Buffy thought that even if there happened to be a
nasty fox, all the others in the forest were nice and kind.

For an hour they looked everywhere. But it didn't
help. They found no Evert and no Karen. Not even the
smallest trace.

"What shall we do?" Gordon paced anxiously back
and forth.

He who was always so calm and collected. He who
always knew what the police must do. Now he was
uncertain, with tears in his eyes. It was just so awful,
having two little ones missing.

He blew his nose into his large handkerchief.

"We need to interrogate the children again," said Buffy.

"Difficult," said Gordon. "They're so shy."

"I'll have to *play* with them," said Buffy. "And talk a little."

"Hmm," said Gordon. "I don't quite understand..."

They hurried back to the kindergarten.

"Let's take off our police hats," said Buffy.

She went to the playroom and began building with blocks. Gordon sat on the sofa and watched.

The children were still looking for the farmer book. "Fuu-nny faaaar-mer book!" they called in every corner.

Buffy kept building.

"Brrrm, brrrm," she said. "I'm driving my little police car to the kindergarten.

The little ones stopped hunting. They came and sat beside her.

"Here come all the children," she said.

Buffy made twelve blocks spill out of the classroom.

One of them stopped. "Hi there. I'm Evert. I'm going to fly a rocket to the moon..."

"I'll come too," said another jumping block. "My name's Karen."

The two blocks clomped away.

Then one of the little ones asked: "Why are they going to the moon?"

"Because we want to," said the Evert block. "We've always wanted to go there."

"What?" said all the real children.

"Hang on," said the Karen block. "I've forgotten… No, I want to be an astronaut. I always say that."

"No you don't!" all the children cried. "You want to be a farmer, Karen."

"And so does Evert!" said the hedgehog.

"What?" said the Evert block. "I've never said that."

"You have so!" said the mole called Elliott. "You're always talking about it!"

Still on the sofa, Chief Detective Gordon took out his notebook. *New interrogation,* he wrote.

Then he crossed out *interrogation* and wrote *game* instead. Then he wrote *farmer.*

Chief Detective Buffy thought. When she'd come across the kindergarten children yesterday, while sitting on the veranda waiting for Gordon, she'd heard some children talking about farmers…

She thought and thought. The children had talked about mud and backpacks. But also about farmers. What had they said? Suddenly she remembered.

Rabbit baby: *Then we can build a house to live in.*

Squirrel baby: *We can be farmers and grow nuts…*

Rabbit baby: *Nuts, yuck. Carrots are better. And we should plant cakes!*

It was Evert and Karen she'd heard!

She went over and told Gordon what she remembered.

"A good interrogation!" Gordon was a little subdued. "You're good at remembering things. Much better than I, Chief Detective Buffy!"

Buffy blushed. She was pretty good, in fact. Almost a police genius…

"Are you going to the moon now?" all the children called out.

Buffy hurried back and picked up the Evert and Karen blocks.

"Where do you think we should go?"

"To the place in the book!" said the magpie baby.

"Now I've forgotten which book it was," said Buffy, scratching her head.

"The faaar-mer book!" everyone called out.

Buffy and Gordon looked at each other.

Oh, the farmer book. In it was a clue that could tell them where the children had gone. But it had disappeared!

What should the police chiefs do?

Gordon wrote in his notebook:

? ? ?

CHAPTER SEVEN

Wait, wait

Far, far away in the forest there was a rustling amongst the leaves. Two little ones came walking along a path. Both wore backpacks and floral tops. And each one carried a stick. The one in the lead shouted and sang the song she'd made up.

Two happy farmers on their way
To work in the fields every day
And eat the cakes that grow there.

The one following seemed a little anxious.
"Will we find it?" he asked. "Is it a long way?"
"I always find everything," she answered.
"We can run to make it shorter!"
She bounced away along the path.
And he scuttled after her.

Yes, it was Karen and Evert! On their way to the place where they'd be farmers. And they almost knew where it was. Almost.

First there was the path through the forest. Then they'd come to the stream.

But phew, phew, the path through the forest was long and twisty.

Suddenly Evert stopped.

"Is that dangerous?" he asked.

They stood puffing for a moment. Their feet were wet because the grass was wet. They were starting to feel a little cold.

But it was a sunny and beautiful autumn day and everything seemed so peaceful in the forest. Except for the rustling all around them. Yellow leaves floated from the trees. Now and then they heard a little thud.

"What is it?" said Evert. "Something dangerous?"

Thud, thud.

"Nothing dangerous," said Karen.

"What about the fox?" whispered Evert.

Thud, thud, thud.

Something was falling from the tree. Karen tried to see what was falling. But it went too fast through the air. Then something hit her on the head. An acorn.

She picked up the acorn and laughed. "Ha ha, there's nothing dangerous. I told you."

"Acorns, that's good!" said Evert. "We can stay here…"

But Karen was already running.

"Okay, okay, nuts are even better," said Evert, following.

At last the path ended, and there was the stream with a footbridge crossing it. All of the kindergarten children usually balanced on the bridge on their way to the big field. The mouse teacher usually stayed underneath, being a troll.

Evert crept up to the bridge. He looked under it. No, no troll today.

"We're not playing trolls today," he told Karen. "It's a bit too scary."

Karen hopped quickly over the bridge. And Evert crept carefully after her.

"Hmm," said Karen. "Which way now?"

She headed right, towards a dark forest of firs.

"Let's run!" she called.

"No," said Evert. "That's the wrong way."

They stopped and looked around.

"There aren't any cones on the way to the place," said Evert. "I know because I'm a squirrel."

They caught sight of the great big tree a little further on.

Yes, it was that way! Left instead.

Karen ran in front. They'd reached the big field. There was the lake. And the tallest tree in the whole forest. This is where they'd have their little farm.

First they used their sticks to dig the ground. It was a shame they didn't have a proper spade. That would make it much easier. But anyway, they got rid of all the grass. The earth beneath was black and soft.

Then they looked in their backpacks.

A little bag of carrot seeds. Seven hazelnuts. A bag of wheat. And two mugs.

They hummed as they planted everything in the dark earth. Then they went down to the lake and filled their mugs with water.

They sat beside the garden plot and watched.

They watched and waited. At first nothing happened. But then they saw something curling beneath the soil.

"Something's coming!" Karen cried.

"Shh!" whispered Evert, bending closer.

Yes, something was coming up out of the earth. A carrot or a whole tree?

A little worm came slithering up.

"A worm," Evert said, disappointed. "It should be carrots, nuts, and cakes! Maybe we did it wrong."

He dug in his backpack and pulled out a book. He leafed through it.

No, they'd done everything right.

"Here's the page that says *wait, wait*," he said.

"Well, we must have to wait a bit longer," said Karen. "But I'm really hungry for cake."

Evert held the farming book in his arms. They sat in the big field and looked at the black earth. And waited.

CHAPTER EIGHT

Sieve, sieve
Bake a cake

The farming book had disappeared from the classroom. What was it about? And what places did it mention?

Gordon cleared his throat.

"Listen to me, children! Can anyone tell me what was inside the book, the so-called funny farmer book?"

Gordon was sounding gruff again. Buffy couldn't understand why. Had he completely forgotten how to be a police officer while he was away? Was he a little nervous now he was back?

The little ones shot under the table and watched fearfully from between the chair legs.

Buffy gave her friend an anxious look.

"Hmm," said Gordon. "Perhaps you'd better take over."

Buffy thought. How could she get the children to tell her what was in the book? Yes! That was it.

"Come, come. We have to write the book again. And draw it!"

And so all the children rushed off to fetch their crayons. They sat at the table and Buffy gave them a pile of paper.

"Now we'll each draw a page," said Buffy. "Then we'll have great fun reading your book."

The children whispered together

"I'll draw *sieve, sieve*," said a squirrel.

"And I'll draw *everyone happy*," said the magpie baby.

They filled the paper with figures and swirls and dots. The chiefs went around the table and looked at what was appearing.

"Hmm. I actually can't tell what that is…"

Buffy ignored his muttering. "Oh, what a lovely sun!" she told a baby toad.

"That's not a sun," the baby toad said crossly. "It's a cake."

"And there are two small cones," she said to Elliot.

"No!" Elliot snorted. "Those are farmers."

"Hmm," said Gordon, smiling a little.

Some of the children worked so quickly they did two drawings each.

It was a problem that none of the children could write. But of course they remembered what the teacher said when she read the book and held each page open. And Buffy could write, most words at least. So she asked them to tell her what to write. And she wrote it with a black pen.

At last she had put together the whole book. She read it through.

Wait, wait. Build a house. Everyone happy! Bake a cake. Sow a seed. Over the stream. Make the bed. Sieve, sieve. Dig the field. Off we go. Everyone helps. Find the field.

Buffy read it again carefully. The book was about two cones, sorry, *farmers*, whose methods were pretty slapdash. Higgledy-piggledy. They ran hither and thither. The funny farming book was not especially funny.

Buffy thought and scratched behind her ear. Of course, she realized, the pages aren't in the right order.

So now she asked the children to sort them out.

Buffy then read aloud to everyone.

Off we go. Over the stream. Find the field. Dig the field. Sow a seed. Wait, wait. Build a house. Make the bed. Sieve, sieve. Bake a cake. Everyone helps. Everyone happy!

Now it was much clearer. It was the story of two farmers who found a place where they could dig a field. They sowed seeds and harvested. There was a lot of waiting, but they built a house and made the bed while they waited. Then when the flour was ground, they sieved the flour and baked and ate a cake and were very happy.

But where was this place? Over a stream, in a field. But that could be anywhere...

Buffy and Gordon thought and thought. They went back to Evert and Karen's boxes. They took out all Karen's drawings again.

"What are those?" said Gordon. "Dots?"

"Seeds!" Buffy said. "She's drawn lots
and lots of seeds. And the long orange
sausages are carrots that are ready to eat!"

Then they pulled out Evert's box of cones.

"Farmers!" said Gordon triumphantly.

Yes, Evert had made lots of farmers out of cones.
Sweaty farmers, farmers working, happy farmers in
caps. And one who was cross because he'd lost his cap...

"Evert and Karen thought about farmers all the
time," said Buffy. "They wanted to be farmers."

"But where is this place?"

They went back to the table where all the drawing
had been done. And then Buffy found it! One drawing
had slipped under the table. A drawing of something big
and green.

"What a lovely flower," said Buffy.

"No, *highest tree*," all the children called at once.

Now it all made sense. *Over the stream. Highest tree.
Find the field.* On the other side of the stream, there
should be a field with the highest tree—the very tallest
tree in the forest...

"I know!" shouted Buffy and Gordon at the same time.

CHAPTER NINE

An important discussion on which police should do what

Both chiefs knew exactly. There was a big field with a very tall tree.

Karen and Evert had heard the story a hundred times. And they badly wanted to do the same thing. They must have been thinking of that very field.

Gordon went at once to put on his gold police hat.

"I shall go right away and look for them," he said formally.

What? What did he mean? Buffy wondered. Why should *he* go? It was Buffy who'd managed to get the children to reveal the place. And it was Buffy who was now Chief of Police!

"Why would you go there on your own?" she asked crossly.

"Well," said Gordon, "because I'm the oldest."

"But I'm the quickest!" Buffy burst out.

"But I've been Chief Detective for many, many years!" said Gordon.

"But I am Chief Detective right at this moment. You're taking a break."

Buffy was hopping mad with old Gordon.

"Then we should both go," said Gordon. "Put on your police hat!"

Buffy snorted. "It's not for you to decide when I put on my police hat!"

"Yes it is," said Gordon.

"No," said Buffy. "I'll have my police hat in my hand and it's none of your business."

They glared crossly at each other. The fine old police friends were so angry. And now they were arguing about whether Buffy should have the hat on her head or in her hand...

"Hrmph!" Gordon growled.

"Hragh!" Buffy goaded him. "By the way, all the animals should come to the field. They can bring food and bandages and blankets…"

That was wisely said, thought Gordon. He grew even more bitter because he hadn't thought of it himself.

"Then I'll go out to them," said Gordon, "to explain what we've come up with…"

"You!" squeaked Buffy. "Why should *you* say it? I want to say it!"

"No," said Gordon. "*I* want to say it."

For a long time they stood glaring at each other.

"Stupid old toad!"

"Idiot child!" said Gordon.

"Eeeeeh!" Buffy squealed. "Old fat-head. Eeeh!"

"Grrruff," Gordon rasped. "Don't use bad words in nursery school! Grrr."

The good old friends. The finest of characters. The sharpest of thinkers. The cream of the police! Now they stood there making strange noises. Why?

Then the baby mole Elliot came forward and stood between them.

"This is not nursery school," he said in his little voice. "Only old people call it that. It's actually called kindergarten. And here in kindergarten we're supposed to be friendly and kind to each other."

"Hmph," said both Gordon and Buffy.

"Here in kindergarten we say sorry when we've been silly."

"Hmph," they said again.

"And then we sing the sorry song." Elliot held out his hands.

Reluctantly they formed a little ring and circled sulkily. The little mole began to sing.

Look, we've been angry again,
So dance with me, my friend.
Sorry, sorry, sorrrrrr-ry!

After a few turns the chiefs stood sullenly, looking at the floor. Their noses were a little red. They were ashamed.

"And now we pat our cheeks!" said the baby mole. "That's what we do here after the sorry song."

Gordon reached out and patted the soft fur beside Buffy's whiskers. Buffy stroked her little hand over Gordon's cheek, which was surprisingly smooth in spite of its wrinkles.

"I was a bit stupid," said Gordon, looking at the ground. "It's a while since I was a real police officer, the kind who thinks of others and never gets angry. And the mice called you a clever and stylish police officer. And you were so very good at the interrogation. To be honest, I was a little jealous. And there's one more thing I haven't told you…"

"I was stupid too," Buffy interrupted with a squeak.

"And I'll never call you an old toad again."

"Now you're being clever and grown up!" said Elliot.

Then they both tried not to cry. But Gordon managed to salute in a very proper way. Buffy did too.

"Finest police chief!" said Gordon with a lump in his throat.

"Wisest detective!" said Buffy and her voice broke into a squeak.

So they decided to go out together and ask everyone to join their expedition to the field. Because now they really were in a hurry! But Gordon took the time to write a brief report in his notebook.

An important discussion on what police shall do was completed. Police shall not compete. And it is very good that they are different.

Far, far away in the big field, Karen and Evert had just built a house.

It wasn't exactly as they'd imagined. They'd wanted to build a square house out of wooden boards, with a little window, a lovely door and a chimney.

But how could they? They had only leaves and sticks to build with.

When the house was finished it looked more like
a pile of leaves with a pointed top. Something an old
man might have raked together. But at least they could
go inside the leaf pile through a hole.

Inside the house, they should have two beds to make.
But the beds were also small piles of leaves. Karen
scratched her head. She couldn't figure out how to
make them.

She flattened them a little.

"There," she said. "Built house. Made beds. Just like in the farmer book."

Afterwards they sat by the field and waited, waited.

The little worm that had worked its way out of the earth had squirmed away.

But nothing else had come up. No matter how hard they stared.

"I hear something. Over there!" said Evert. "Could it be the fox?"

But Karen wasn't listening.

"Will the cakes come straight out of the ground?" she asked instead. "And what sort will they be? Vanilla? Meringue?"

Evert said he didn't think they'd grow straight up. That way they'd have dirt on them. And cakes didn't usually.

"Strawberry!" said Karen. "I think they'll be strawberry cakes."

Evert looked it up in the book.

"*Sieve, sieve. Bake a cake* is on this page," he said. "You have to do the sieving first…"

At kindergarten they'd learned to sieve sand in the sandpit. And then they'd baked cakes.

"That's what we'll do then!" Karen said.

So they went off to look. Down by the stream,
they found a beach with fine sand.

"Isn't it dangerous here?" asked Evert.

Karen wasn't listening. She was singing a little song.

Rescue expedition

The rescue expedition set off in the afternoon.

Possibly. Neither Gordon nor Buffy had any idea what time it was. They were ravenously hungry. They hadn't eaten anything all day. And because they hadn't eaten any cakes, they didn't know if it was time for a morning cake, an afternoon cake, or an evening cake.

The rescue expedition marched on its way.

The chiefs had asked everyone not to mention the word "fox." This was to avoid frightening anyone unnecessarily.

Gordon and Buffy went first, with their rumbling stomachs and gold caps. They sang the police parade march. Evert's mother and father were on their heels. Then Karen's mother with a swarm of babies around her.

After them came seven rabbits with seven blankets, in case Karen and Evert were freezing.

Then came twelve mice carrying a large jug of hot chocolate.

"Good and warming if you're frozen," said one of the mouse mothers.

Then came three hedgehogs with bandages, in case the two children had been snagged by something sharp and thorny.

Then came five moles with spades in their hands, in case the missing children were stuck in a pit.

After them flew eleven crows with long ropes in their beaks, in case the pit was very deep.

Three badgers carried a ladder, in case they'd climbed a tree and couldn't get down.

Sixteen field voles carried a big jug of hot chocolate.

A father vole said:

"Good and warming if… What? Have the mice brought hot chocolate too?"

Thirteen water voles carried a bag of newly baked buns and cakes, in case Karen and Evert were hungry.

Two otters carried a thick cushion, in case they wanted to go straight to sleep.

What a long procession this rescue mission made! And it was still going.

Next came two lizards carrying soap, in case they were dirty.

They were followed by four toads with towels, in case they needed to dry themselves afterwards.

And then came two toads with dry underwear and socks, in case there had been a small accident.

Then another four badgers carrying a little boat, in case they had gone too far out on the lake.

Seven magpies with a fire extinguisher. In case of fire.

Thirty-two gulls with a net. In case the young ones…

"Well, you never know," said the gulls. "There might be a you-know-what there."

Finally, a group of thirty-seven animals brought a little of everything. Dice, crayons, a paper dart a little buckled from crashing, three flowers, a broken cup, a funny lump of clay, and something no one could identify…

In total, one hundred and eighty animals followed the chiefs.

Then came the ten kindergarten children and their teacher. They had flowery tops and sticks in their hands. The teacher was carrying the new book they had made together. And they were singing their song.

Two songs were sung about the rescue mission. One at the front and one at the back. But it didn't matter because their line was so long they didn't disturb one another.

Now the whole procession was stretched over the footbridge.

Buffy suddenly called out.

"STOP!"

Everyone stopped. They hurried over to hear what had happened.

Buffy stood there sniffing. Then she suddenly looked worried.

"Something smells tragic and terrible," she said.

"What?" they all cried.

"It smells of death," she said. "Someone has just died here."

At once it was so quiet you could hear leaves falling through the air and softly landing on the ground.

Then a very old crow called out:

"No-ooo, this means the fox has eaten the little ones!"

Gordon and Buffy gave the crow a sharp look. Then they said together:

"Stop your croaking. We police officers will go and investigate."

While the chiefs crept forwards, the hundred and eighty animals stood perfectly still, hardly daring to breathe.

Buffy sniffed and showed the way.

And there was a dead body.

Gordon put his hand to his heart and sighed deeply.

The chiefs took off their police hats and bent their heads.

It was a lark. A very old lark on the way to fly south had suddenly died.

"Always sang so beautifully, but now silent," said Gordon ceremoniously. "Sad, but such is life…"

The police told the others what had happened.

Unfortunately there was no time for a burial. But the three moles with spades stayed behind and saw to it. The moles were very good at digging. And good at singing dark and gloomy songs.

The rescue mission was able to leave three flowers and the funny lump of clay as a decoration for the grave.

The expedition hurried on its way, and soon they had reached the big field.

"I have the feeling something terrible's happened," croaked the old crow ominously.

CHAPTER ELEVEN

Everyone helps!

In the big field sat two lonely children.

"Help!" called little Evert.

They were scared. Nothing had gone as they'd hoped.

First they had left the field and the newly built house, or pile of leaves it looked more like. They'd gone down to the edge of the lake and found some fine sand. They'd carried back as much as they could in their cupped hands.

Then they had sat in front of the new house, or pile of leaves, and begun to sieve the sand. Karen said that you took the sand in your hands, then you rubbed your hands together while you said "kshee, kshee, kshee." And the sand that sifted down to the ground was freshly sieved flour ready to bake with.

The two of them sat quite a long time sieving sand.

In fact they were just sieving extra flour while they waited for something to grow. But they'd forgotten that. Suddenly they were baking cakes out of sand, just like they always did at kindergarten. And then they forgot that they weren't baking real cakes.

And they were really hungry. Evert put a whole sand cake in his mouth. Karen was even hungrier and put two sand cakes in at once.

There was some terrible spitting and spluttering. Yuck, it's so hard getting rid of sand when it's stuck to your tongue!

There sat two lonely children.

Evert was crying. They were both freezing and very miserable. Their dream of being farmers had fallen apart.

"Help!" called little Evert.

And just then he heard a clompety-clomp from the edge of the forest. He thought at least a hundred foxes were coming to eat him up…

Clompety-clompety-clomp. Closer and closer it came. And a song could be heard.

Look, the forest police are here!
The brave police …

Suddenly Evert and Karen caught sight of two gold police caps. And they had never seen so many grownups in one place in all their life.

"Mamma, papa, mamma!" called Evert and Karen.

The entire rescue expedition marched into the field: two mothers and one father, police, all the different animals, hot chocolate, a boat, a ladder, a rope, buns, a broken cup. And something no one could identify.

The entire rescue mission! They filled the field. Everyone stared at the two lost children. And then they all began to cry from happiness and joy. Karen's mother cried hardest of all, even though she'd said she didn't usually worry. The chiefs and the teacher sniffed and sighed, relieved that everything had turned out all right.

The only ones who were any use were the children. They hurried over to Evert and Karen. They put blankets around their shoulders and poured them hot chocolate, gave them buns and cakes, and showed them all the new books at once. And Elliot put on bandages even though they weren't really needed.

What luck that the children were so clever!

Evert and Karen were very surprised by all the goings-on. Karen said the same thing to everyone who hugged her.

"We're farmers. We're farmers."

Buffy wanted to explain something important to all the children.

"Should you do everything you read about in books? I might read about a mouse with wings who can fly. Should I climb a pine tree and leap out into the air?"

"No!" called the children.

"Or I might read about a toad who ate up a fox," said Gordon. "Shall I go out and look for a tasty fox?"

"No no!" they shrieked.

"How can a toad eat a fox?" asked Buffy, because she hadn't heard the answer in the book.

"With butter and a little parsley!" answered Gordon. "Ha ha."

Then they all headed for home. The little runaways sat up in the boat that was carried by the badgers. They had blankets around them and read the books all the way as they swayed above the procession.

"Everyone helps!" said Karen and Evert. "I knew everyone would help!"

"Everyone happy," said Evert to Karen.

Eventually the chiefs had completed their work. They went and got all Gordon's things from the little house. And at last they stepped into the police station.

"Welcome," said Buffy. "Very welcome back again!"

"It's been a long time," said Gordon, putting his police hat on the hat shelf. "It looks just the way it did."

They sat down at the desk. Buffy put on the kettle and began to take out the cakes. Morning cakes, lunch cakes...

Then she looked out the window. Yes, the sun was going down. It was time for evening cakes too. It was a very big plateful. But they also had very empty stomachs.

We had a case in any case, Gordon thought happily. Now I must write down something important.

He sat and hummed for a while and then he read what he'd written.

```
There are so many things to be afraid
of. But there are so many good and kind
animals who want to help. And we can't
say that even one of them is wicked...
```

Buffy nodded. At least one hundred and eighty good
and kind animals. Not one wicked.

"Will you stamp this important piece of paper?"
asked Gordon. "Because it's your stamp."

But Buffy said they must eat first and stamp later.

"I have a present for you after that," said Buffy.
"But first the cakes. Come and help yourself!"

On the plate were walnut balls, strawberry drops, and sugar bombs.

First they ate the morning cakes, then the strawberry drops they should have had for lunch, and finally the evening sugar bombs. Then their stomachs were so full they had to lie down in bed.

"I'm so happy that you came to get me," said Gordon sleepily.

"Were you really pleased that I woke you?" asked Buffy.

"Yes," said Gordon. "The best thing is when someone needs you. When you can help!"

"Of course, it's also best when nothing happens

at the police station," said Buffy. "No wrongdoing, nothing terrible. Just peace and quiet."

"Yes," said Gordon, yawning a little.

"But next best is when two police officers can solve a mystery together."

"Yes," said Gordon.

"So that everyone's happy!"

"Yes," said Gordon, with a big yawn.

"And you and I are really best friends!"

"Yes," said Gordon. "It was very tedious on my own. I'm so glad I was needed. And that you came and woke…SNORK."

Right there, mid sentence, Gordon fell asleep and began to snore especially noisily.

"Yes," said Buffy. "Now we just need to find out what the mysterious scrabbler wants."

She got up. She had something important to do before she went to bed.

Fix the flour bomb! And the present.

Everyone should
sleep happy

When Buffy was finished at last with her preparations,
she went into the old prison. There lay Gordon with
his clothes on, snoring like a small fat piglet.

Buffy was worried. The mysterious scrabbler had
turned up two nights in a row. She didn't want to
sleep on her own. The other bed was in the other
room. Using all her strength, Buffy moved it in beside
Gordon's. Even when the bed legs screeched across the
floor, Gordon didn't wake.

She changed into her nightie and went to bed.

She still felt uneasy, and thoughts swarmed through her head. What did the ghost want? Would the flour bomb work? Was it a fox…

SNORK.

Suddenly she was asleep anyway. In the middle of a thought.

Buffy dreamed that she and Gordon argued and poked their tongues out at one another. Gordon dreamed at the same time that he'd lied so terribly that his tongue turned as black as chocolate cake.

He woke with a heavy, ominous feeling. Buffy slept soundly in the bed beside him.

A breath of fresh air was what he needed! But it was raining outside. He put on his boots and pulled a raincoat out of his suitcase.

Then he stood outside the window and breathed deeply. Rain, rain. His boots squelched. He slid a little and then, catching his balance, leaned against the window.

Buffy dreamed about the lovely present and…

Scrabble scrabble.

Suddenly she woke to the terrible scuffling noise, in the middle of her dream. Had the ghost come? The fox! It was time for the flour bomb plan!

Buffy scampered out of bed and hurried over to the

back window. She climbed out. She'd hidden her flour bomb under a garden chair. It was for scaring off the fox. She took it in her arms.

The flour bomb was a blown-up balloon half full of flour, with a peg at the top so nothing would leak out.

She hurried around the police station. The balloon was pretty heavy. Now the fox would get a surprise. Flour in its eyes!

Buffy lifted the flour bomb and shook it. The flour became a cloud inside the balloon.

She approached the mysterious figure, ready to take off the peg. What a surprise for that fox.

With a farty hiss, a cloud of flour sprayed over the dark, lumpy figure.

"Help!" the figure shouted. "In the name of the law!"

And it coughed. And got flour in its mouth. And was white as a ghost.

Yes, there stood a white, ghostly Gordon. And beside him was Buffy with the little empty balloon in her hand.

"What!" said Buffy. "Are you the one who's been creeping around here at night?"

"Phoof," said Gordon, rubbing his eyes. "I was just

keeping watch out here. It's been so tedious and I missed my police work. And you were going to whistle for me if you needed me. You promised…"

"But I wanted to show you how good I was at managing on my own," said Buffy.

"Hmm. Let's not talk any more about it."

Buffy brushed Gordon down.

"Police should always help each other," said Buffy.

Then they saluted several times. Buffy danced back inside. They sat down at the writing desk. Gordon hunted out some old secret night cakes. Dark chocolate clouds, he called them. Wonderfully good!

"However, now we must write a report!" he said.

```
      The case of the scrabbler:
  the "crime" was missing and longing.
    The flour bomb solved everything.
```

"Very good summary," said Buffy. "But those who don't know what happened won't understand much."

"But you and I understand, my dear Buffy," said Gordon. "And I shall sternly tell myself never to be stupid and angry again."

They shared the last chocolate cloud.

"Now I have a surprise for you," said Buffy.

She went and got the present that she had made.
She dragged it into the room.

It was a whopping stamp that took two to lift, and
two to stamp with.

It was round and had the royal crown. *Detective
Gordon and Detective Buffy* it said.

"You are a genius," said Gordon. "A police genius."

"And you are very wise," said Buffy. "A wise police
officer."

"Great to be able to stamp again," said Gordon.
"Once a police officer, always a police officer."

They lifted the stamp up onto the desk.

"All cases are solved!" they said.

They placed the stamp on the report. Moved it a little to the right, a little to the left. KLA-BOOM! They stamped so the whole desk shook.

A big stamp. Two police. Two happy friends.

And when the sun came up, they crept back to bed. Gordon immediately began to snore, puffing out small clouds of flour.

Buffy smiled and felt very happy. She whispered to herself:

"Everyone should sleep happy. Good night! Good morning!"

POLICE
STATION

Who is the
mysterious
scrabbler?

Flour bomb

BIG STREAM

Nursery School
Kindergarten

SMALL
FIELD

Gordon stays here
on his break

Map of
Detective Gordon
and Detective Buffy's
police district

DETECTIVE GORDON · DETECTIVE BUFFY

HIGHEST TREE

Sometimes there is a troll under the little bridge

The dead lark's grave

BIG FIELD

A house with two newly made beds. Sort of...

This is where cakes should grow. Strawberry cakes?

This edition first published in 2017 by Gecko Press
PO Box 9335, Marion Square, Wellington 6141, New Zealand
info@geckopress.com

English language edition © Gecko Press Ltd 2017

Original title: *Kommisarie Gordon: Ett fall i alla fall*
Text © Ulf Nilsson 2016
Illustrations © Gitte Spee 2016
First published by Bonnier Carlsen, Stockholm, Sweden
Published in the English language by arrangement with
Bonnier Rights, Stockholm, Sweden

Distributed in the United States and Canada by Lerner Publishing Group,
www.lernerbooks.com
Distributed in the United Kingdom by Bounce Sales and Marketing,
www.bouncemarketing.co.uk
Distributed in Australia by Scholastic Australia,
www.scholastic.com.au
Distributed in New Zealand by Upstart Distribution,
www.upstartpress.co.nz

The cost of this translation was defrayed by a subsidy from the
Swedish Arts Council, gratefully acknowledged.

Translated by Julia Marshall
Edited by Penelope Todd
Typesetting by Vida & Luke Kelly, New Zealand
Printed in China by Everbest Printing Co Ltd,
an accredited ISO 14001 & FSC certified printer

Hardback (USA) ISBN: 978-1-776571-08-6
Paperback ISBN: 978-1-776571-09-3
Ebook available

For more curiously good books, visit www.geckopress.com